W9-CIG-117

Dear Parent:

Congratulations! Your child is taking the first steps on an exciting journey. The destination? Independent reading!

STEP INTO READING® will help your child get there. The program offers five steps to reading success. Each step includes fun stories and colorful art. There are also Step into Reading Sticker Books, Step into Reading Math Readers, Step into Reading Phonics Readers, Step into Reading Write-In Readers, and Step into Reading Phonics Boxed Sets—a complete literacy program with something for every child.

Learning to Read, Step by Step!

Ready to Read   Preschool–Kindergarten
• big type and easy words • rhyme and rhythm • picture clues
For children who know the alphabet and are eager to begin reading.

Reading with Help   Preschool–Grade 1
• basic vocabulary • short sentences • simple stories
For children who recognize familiar words and sound out new words with help.

Reading on Your Own   Grades 1–3
• engaging characters • easy-to-follow plots • popular topics
For children who are ready to read on their own.

Reading Paragraphs   Grades 2–3
• challenging vocabulary • short paragraphs • exciting stories
For newly independent readers who read simple sentences with confidence.

Ready for Chapters   Grades 2–4
• chapters • longer paragraphs • full-color art
For children who want to take the plunge into chapter books but still like colorful pictures.

STEP INTO READING® is designed to give every child a successful reading experience. The grade levels are only guides. Children can progress through the steps at their own speed, developing confidence in their reading, no matter what their grade.

Remember, a lifetime love of reading starts with a single step!

Step into Reading, Random House, and the Random House colophon are registered trademarks of Random House, Inc.

Visit us on the Web!
StepIntoReading.com
randomhouse.com/kids

Educators and librarians, for a variety of teaching tools, visit us at RHTeachersLibrarians.com

ISBN 978-0-449-81857-2 (trade) — ISBN 978-0-449-81858-9 (lib. bdg.)
Printed in the United States of America
10 9 8 7 6 5 4 3 2 1

STEP INTO READING®

STEP 1

nickelodeon

DORA the EXPLORER

Dora's Puppy, Perrito!

By Mary Tillworth

Illustrated by Dave Aikins

Random House 🏠 New York

Dora has a puppy.

His name is Perrito.

Dora loves to play
with her puppy!

Dora and Boots
visit Dora's grandmother.

Dora's grandmother
has a gift for Perrito!

Dora says thank you
to her grandmother.

Now Dora and Boots
must get home.
They check Map.

First,
Dora and Boots go
to Butterfly Garden.

Swiper has
a robot butterfly.
He wants to swipe
the gift!

Dora sees Swiper.

"Swiper, no swiping!"

she says.

Dora and Boots

cross a bridge.

The wind blows
the gift away.
The gift flies
into the river!

15

Dora uses a fishing pole.

She hooks the gift!

Dora and Boots
go to the Dancing Trees.

They count the trees.

There are ten!

Dora and Boots

wave their arms.

They look like trees.

They dance the

Tree Dance!

Swiper dresses

like a tree.

He sneaks

past Dora and Boots.

Swiper swipes the gift!

"Swiper, no swiping! That's Perrito's gift," says Dora.

Swiper loves puppies!

He gives the gift back.

Dora and Boots
walk home.
They see Perrito!

The puppy wags
his tail.

Dora and Boots open
Perrito's gift.

There is a bowl.

There is a collar.

There is a leash.

There is a bone!

Dora puts
the collar
and the leash
on Perrito.

Perrito chews

on the bone.

He loves it!

Dora loves her puppy!